One Christmas Day, Tim's pr[...]
a rocking horse,
an airplane,
a train,
and Rabbit.

Rabbit was his best present.
It had big, soft ears
and dark brown spots.

"Come on, Rabbit."
Off they went on the white rocking horse.
"Faster, faster!" Tim laughed.

Up they flew in the blue airplane.
Rabbit was the pilot.
"Let's go," Tim said.

Off they went on the red train.
"Rabbit, you're a real friend," Tim said.

One morning, Rabbit looked at Tim.
Mom looked at Tim.
"Oh, Tim! YOU have spots."

The doctor came.
"Tim, you are very sick. All your toys
have to go!"

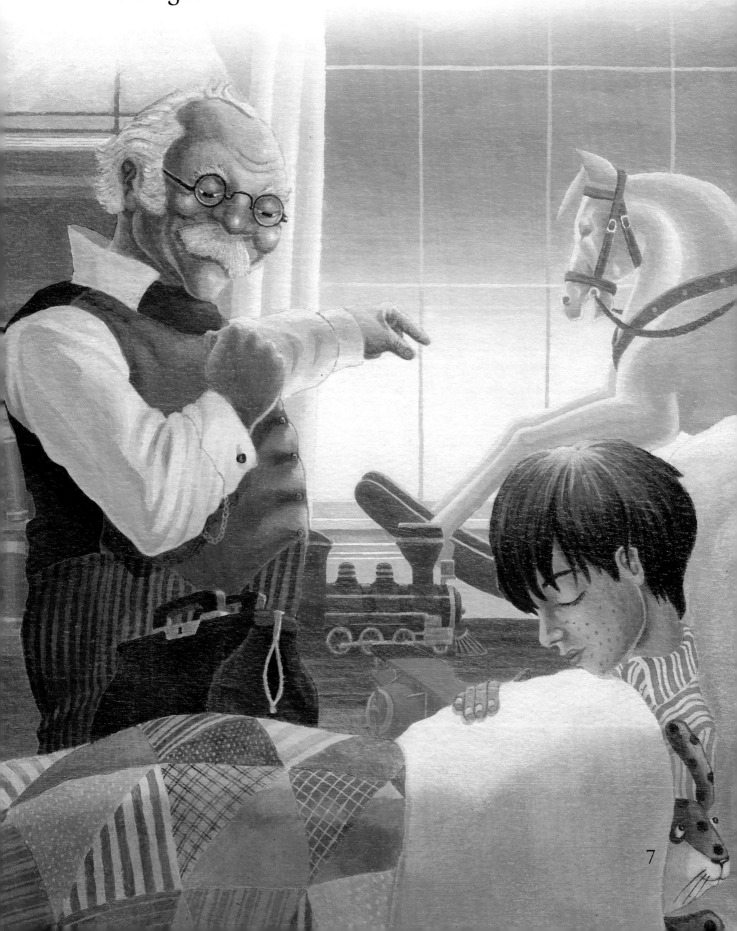

Mom put all Tim's toys in a sack.
She put the sack in the garden.

Rabbit was very cold and very sad.
But that night some real rabbits came.

9

Rabbit wanted to play with the rabbits.
"But I can't, I'm a toy," he said.

"You can!" a fairy said.
"You were real to Tim.
Now, you're a real rabbit!"

One day Tim said,
"Look, no more spots, Mom. Can I play
in the garden?"

"Look Mom. That rabbit looks like my toy Rabbit. He has dark brown spots!"

Mom looked. "That's a real rabbit, Tim."
"My Rabbit was real to me," Tim said.

ACTIVITIES

BEFORE YOU READ

1. Look at the cover of the book. What can you see?
   (a) a gray rabbit with white spots.
   (b) a brown rabbit with dark brown spots.
   (c) a pink rabbit with white spots.

2. Look in the book. Can you find:
   a sack   a rocking horse   a fairy
   a real rabbit   a toy rabbit?

AFTER YOU READ

3. Look at the pictures of the toys in the story. Match the toy to the right color.

It's blue!
It's white!
It's red!

Pearson Education Limited
Edinburgh Gate, Harlow
Essex CM20 2JE, England
and Associated Companies throughout the world.

ISBN 978-0-582-77858-0

This adaptation first published by
Penguin Books 2003

7 9 10 8

The Velveteen Rabbit
Level 2
Adapted by Audrey McIlvain
Series Editor: Melanie Williams
Series created by Annie Hughes and Melanie Williams

Design by Shireen Nathoo Design
Colour reproduction by Spectrum Colour, Ipswich
Printed in China
SWTC/07

Published by Pearson Education Limited in association with Penguin Books Ltd,
both companies being subsidiaries of Pearson Plc

For a complete list of titles available in the Penguin Young Readers series
please write to your local Pearson Education office or contact:
Penguin Readers Marketing Department, Pearson Education, Edinburgh Gate,
Harlow, Essex, CM20 2JE.

**Answers for the Activities in this book are published in the free
Penguin Young Readers Factsheet on the website, www.penguinreaders.com**